Maths Adventures
Firefighters to the Rescue

 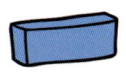 

By John Allan

Contents

Welcome to the Fire Station	4
Your Fire Station	6
Starting Your Shift	8
The Alarm Call	10
How Fast Can They Go?	12
Forest Fire	14
On the Engine	16
Rescue Mission	18
Putting the Fire Out	20
Cleanup Time	22
After Work: Keeping Fit	24
In the News	26
Safety First	28
Tips and Help	30
Answers	32

ISBN 978-1-913077-11-2

Copyright © 2020 Hungry Tomato Ltd
First published in Great Britain in 2020
by Hungry Tomato Ltd,
F1, Old Bakery Studios,
Blewetts Wharf, Malpas Road,
Truro, Cornwall, TR1 1QH
United Kingdom

Welcome to the Fire Station

A firefighter puts out fires and rescues people in trouble. The job is dangerous. Skills and bravery are needed to save lives.

WHAT DOES A FIREFIGHTER DO?

 Firefighters put out fires in homes, stores, and offices.

 Firefighters are usually the first responders to all fires.

 They tell people how fires start and what they can do to prevent them.

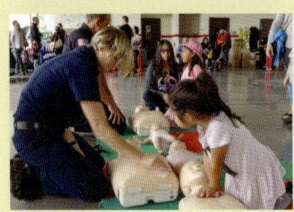 Sometimes they talk to children about their job.

You will need paper, a pencil, and a ruler. Don't forget to wear your firefighter's uniform! Let's go...

What's inside the book?

Find out what needs to be done next in your busy day.

Look for facts about being a firefighter!

Answer the questions and practice your maths skills.

The charts and tables will help you answer the maths questions.

If you get stuck, there are some tips to help you on pages 30–31.

In this book you will find number puzzles that firefighters have to solve every day. You will also get the chance to answer number questions about fires, firefighters, and fire safety.

Did you know that firefighters use maths?

Your Fire Station

You are a firefighter in one of your town's fire stations. You could be called to a fire at any time. You deal with all sorts of fires.

Here are the numbers of workers at your station.
- 2 fire chiefs: They decide how fires should be put out.
- 2 crew leaders: They organise the firefighters.
- 12 firefighters: They tackle the blaze.

1 If these workers are in two equal teams, how many people are there in each team?

2 Your station is always busy! Last year you put out 130 big fires and 100 small fires. How many more big fires were there than small fires?

3 Your team put out 60 car fires and 15 house fires. What is the total number of car and house fires?

4 How many farmland fires were there last month?

5 How many fires were there altogether last month?

WHERE IS THE FIRE?

This graph shows the number of fires last month.

Starting Your Shift

When you arrive at work there are always things to do, even when there are no fires. You have to make sure that everything on the fire engine is working.

Firefighters are needed night and day. They work in shifts. A shift is the time that a firefighter spends at work. It can be a day shift or a night shift.

6 This week you will work four day shifts. How many days in the week are you not working a day shift?

7 The clock shows the time in the morning when you start work. What time is it?

YESTERDAY'S TIMETABLE

You were not called out to a fire yesterday. Here is what you did instead.

9:00 to 10:30	Checked the engine
10:30 to 11:00	Break
11:00 to 12:00	Training
12:00 to 1:00	Cleaning
1:00 to 2:00	Lunch

8 What were you doing at 10:00?

9 What were you doing at 11:30?

10 What were you doing at 1:15?

THE EQUIPMENT

Today you are checking all of the equipment

11 What is the difference between the number of fire hoses and safety clothes in the storeroom?

12 What is the difference between the number of fire hoses and extinguishers?

14 safety clothes

36 fire hoses

18 extinguishers

Uniforms protect firefighters from the heat. They are also waterproof!

The Alarm Call

Someone has dialed 999. There is a fire in town! The alarm bell at the fire station rings. It only takes 60 seconds for you to leave the station.

13 Which of the maths problems below have the answer 10?

- A: 1+2+3+4
- B: 2+2+2+2+2+2
- C: 180−160
- D: 30−3
- E: 2×5

14 A fire in the country takes 20 minutes to get to. How many groups of 2 in 20?

15 The alarm bell sounds. It takes the firefighters one minute to get to the fire engine and leave the station. It then takes two minutes for them to reach the main road and three minutes for them to arrive at the fire. How long has it been since the alarm bell rang?

WHERE IS THE FIRE?

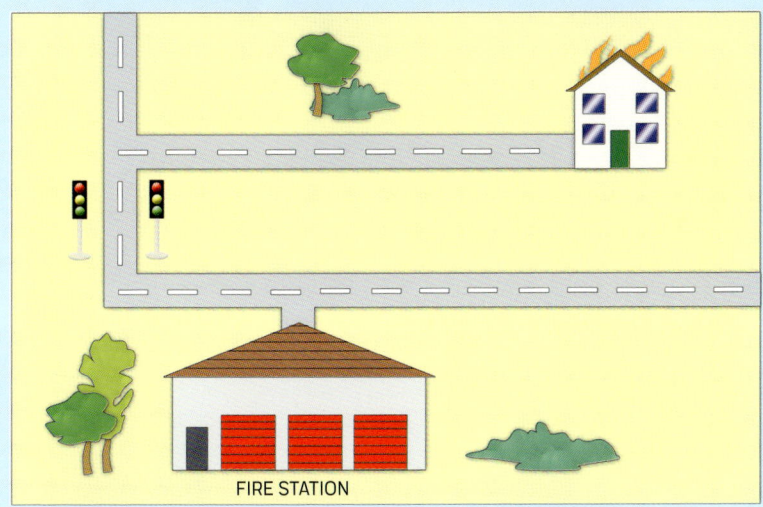

A Turn left out of the station, then left again, go past the traffic lights, and then turn right.

B Turn right out of the station, then left, go past the traffic lights, and then turn left.

C Turn left out of the station, then right, go past the traffic lights, and then turn right.

16 Look at the map of your town. You need to give the driver directions. Would you choose A, B, or C?

How Fast Can They Go?

The fire engine races through traffic. The lights and siren tells other drivers to pull out of the way so the fire engine can get past.

This is the traffic in one lane of a main road.

17 How many vehicles need to pull over to let the fire engine through?

18 The fire engine can go about 3 miles in 3 minutes. How far can it go in 6 minutes?

19 The lights flash 60 times in one minute. How many times do the lights flash in $1\frac{1}{2}$ minutes?

Here is a diagram. It is made of 16 squares.

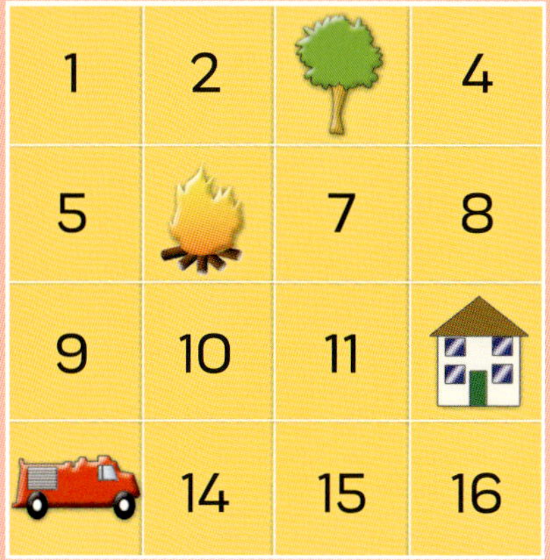

20 What do you find at number 13 on the diagram?

21 What is at number 3 on the diagram?

22 What number is the house on?

23 What is to the left of the number 7 on the map?

1	2	🌳	4
5	🔥	7	8
9	10	11	🏠
🚒	14	15	16

KEY

tree   fire engine   camp fire   house

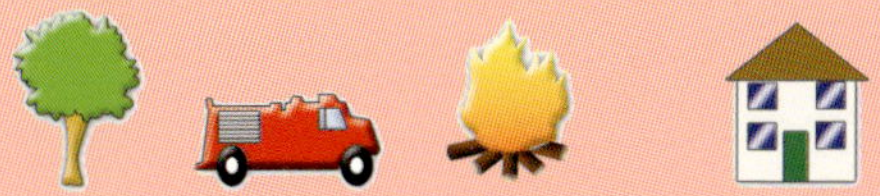

Drivers are specially trained to drive safely at high speeds.

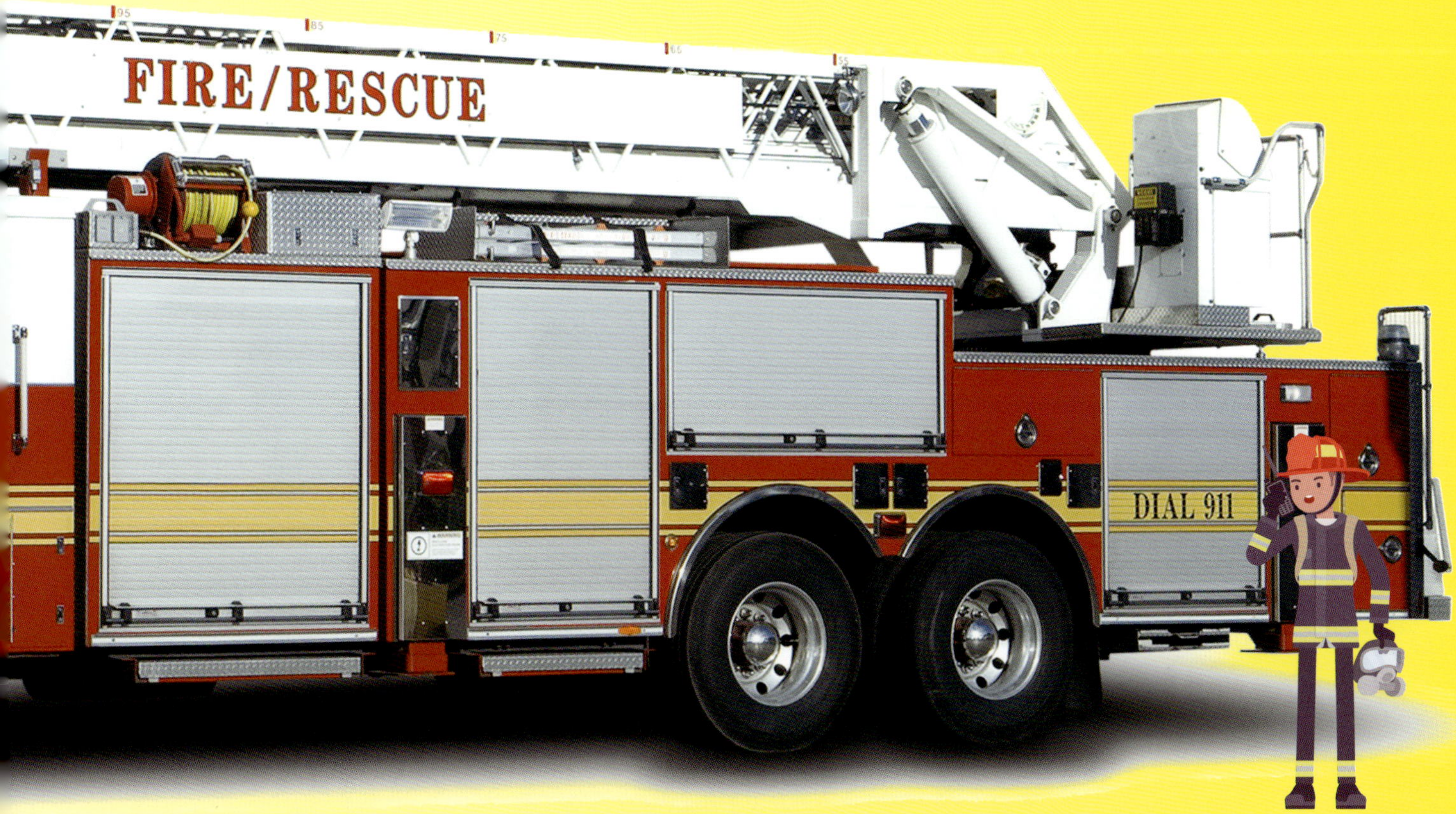

Forest Fire

There is a fire in the woods. The dry wood and leaves mean there is lots of fuel for the fire to burn. A strong wind can make a fire spread very quickly.

Firefighters check the direction of the wind. It is very dangerous to be in front of the fire if the wind is pushing it towards you.

24 Look at Fire A. The wind is blowing from North to South. Is the firefighter safe?

25 At Fire B, the wind is blowing from West to East. Is the firefighter safe?

A FIRE PICTOGRAM

How the fire started	Number of fires
Lightning strike	🔥
Camp fire	🔥🔥🔥🔥🔥
Deliberately started	🔥🔥🔥

 = one fire

Firefighters look for clues to work out how a fire started. Here is a pictogram showing how forest fires started last year.

26 How were most fires started?

27 How many fires were there altogether?

28 Some trees die after a forest fire, but others can recover and grow new leaves in the spring. How many of these trees are burnt?

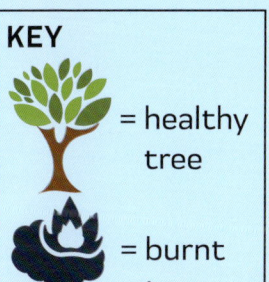

KEY
= healthy tree
= burnt tree

A big wildfire can burn about 2 square kilometres in an hour.

On the Engine

The fire engine has all of the equipment needed to tackle a forest fire. It carries long hoses and ladders as well as 500 gallons of water.

The fire engine's ladders are 20 metres long and 35 metres long.

29 How much higher can the longer ladder reach?

You can see the first eight rungs of this ladder.

30 You are standing on rung 4 and move down 2 steps. What rung are you standing on now?

31 You are on rung 3 and climb up 5 steps. What rung are you on now?

Firefighters make sure a fire is completely out in one area before moving on to the next.

The engine can pump about 10 gallons of water in one second.

32 How much water does it pump in three seconds?

THE WATER TRUCK

As well as engines, the fire station also has a water truck. It can carry over 3000 gallons! That is much more water than the engine can carry.

33 Fire engines have two hoses. Water trucks have five. How many hoses would there be altogether on two fire engines and one water truck?

Rescue Mission

You have arrived at a house fire. Before you can start to fight the fire you need to see where the flames are coming from.

This is the house that has a fire.

34 Name the shapes of the following:
A. roof
B. door
C. top windows
D. window to the left of the door
E. window to the right of the door

There was nobody in the house except for a small dog. Firefighters took:
• 2 minutes to climb the ladder
• 1 minute to lift the dog
• 3 minutes in the house
• 2 minutes to take the dog to safety

35 How long does it take to rescue the small dog?

36 After the rescue, you put the dog on a scale to see how much it weighs. How heavy is the dog?

37 You once carried a small child from a burning building. The child weighed as much as 3 small dogs! How heavy was the child?

38 This is the back of one of your gloves. Is it for your right or left hand?

Your gloves have an inside layer that protect your hands from heat.

Putting the Fire Out

The building is empty, and the flames can be put out. Lots of water is pumped through the hoses.

39 The red hoses are 15 metres long. The yellow hoses are 30 metres long. You can connect them to make a longer hose.

How many of each hose would you use to make a hose that was 45 metres long?

40 How would you make a hose that was 90 metres long? Use the fewest number of hoses.

41 Firefighters can choose the width of the hose as well as its length. This is the smallest hose. Use a ruler to measure the diameter, or distance across the opening **in inches**. How wide is it?

42 Bigger hoses are used to pump more water on to the fire. One is 1.5 inches (3.8 cm) across, and another is 3 inches (7.6 cm) across. Look at this number line. Which letter marks 1.5 inches?

43 What length does the letter E mark?

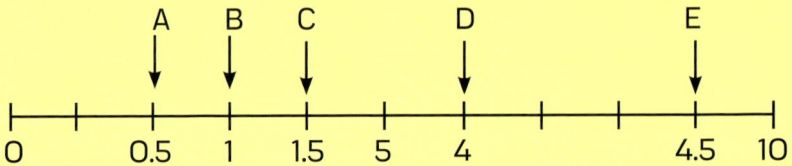

Firefighters respond to emergencies where there is risk to life or property.

Cleanup Time

The fire is out, but is it safe to go back into the building? The team check that there is no chance of another fire starting and that the building won't fall over.

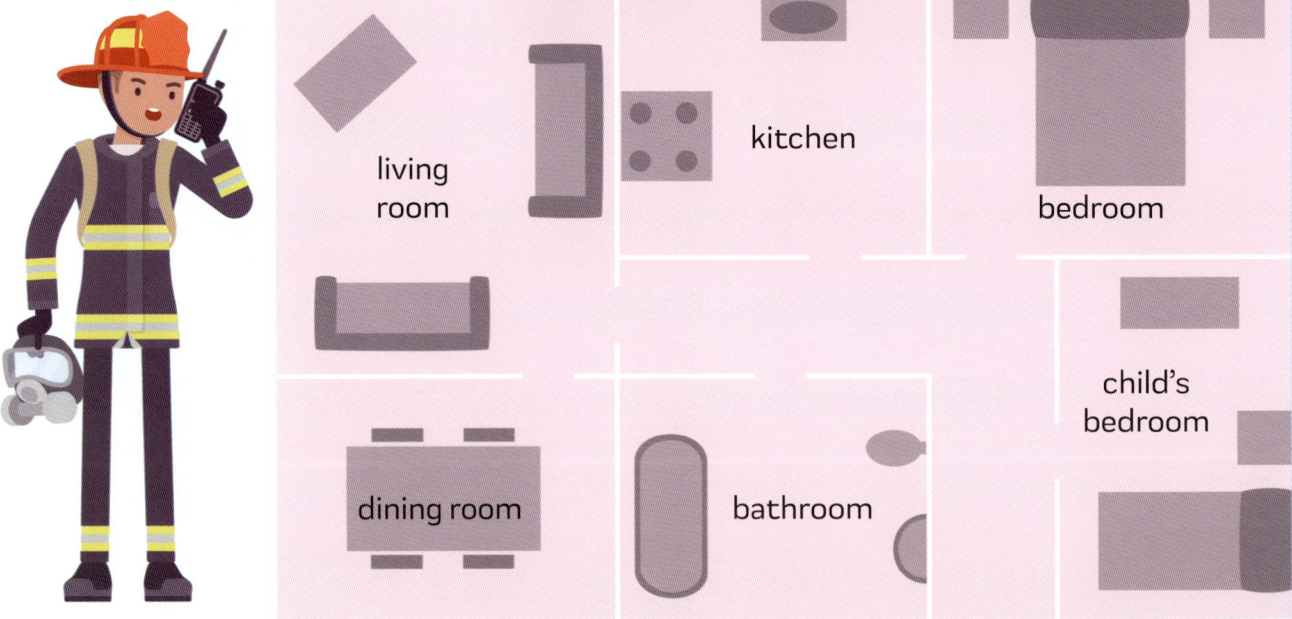

44 This is a plan of the house. You check that the fire is out in every room. How many rooms do you check?

45 You check the kitchen, living room, dining room, and the bathroom. Are you going clockwise or anti-clockwise?

46 How many rooms in this house are bedrooms?

After the fire there are lots of burnt things that need to be thrown away. You fill these items with rubbish:

4 rubbish bins

5 black bags

8 boxes

47 The numbers have been used in these calculations. Can you solve the puzzles?

A
5 + 8

B
8 − 4

C
4 × 5

D
8 ÷ 4

It's not just the fire that destroys homes. The heat, smoke, soot, and water cause damage too.

After Work: Keeping Fit

Firefighters need to keep fit to do their job. They have to bend, stretch, lift, and carry every day. Exercising is vital for a firefighters work.

48 You have hand weights to lift. You need a new set. You want a set that costs less than £17 and weighs less than 5 kg. Which set is best?

	Cost	Weight
Set 1	£10	6 kg
Set 2	£20	8.5 kg
Set 3	£15	4 kg
Set 4	£16	14 kg

49 You have a skipping rope and count your skips. You do 35 skips, rest, and then you do 34. How many in total?

When you exercise, your heart pumps blood around your body quicker. You can check your pulse to find out how fast your heart is beating.

50 Before you start skipping, your heart rate is 75 beats per minute. Afterward, it is up to 92 beats per minute. How many beats has it gone up by?

51 You end your fitness time lying on your mat to relax. Are these sentences true or false?

A. The mat is two metres long.
B. The mat is one metre wide.
C. The width is half of the length.

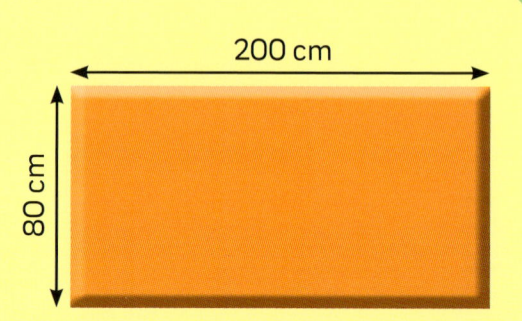

Firefighters must be in shape. The uniform and equipment weigh about 36 kg—and that's before they have to carry anything!

In the News

Big fires are reported in the local newspaper. Read the article and then answer the questions.

YOUR LOCAL NEWS

£1.50 — Every Wednesday & Saturday

People Rescued from Fire!

A brave firefighter rescued five people trapped in a burning building yesterday. The building on York Road caught on fire at seven o'clock last night. Nine firefighters tackled the blaze. They took one hour and eighteen minutes to put the fire out. The people trapped in the building were led to safety by firefighter Helen Jones. Helen, aged twenty-six, has been a firefighter for three years. Helen loves her job, and she has put out forty-eight fires so far.

The fire started at 20 York Road. Two other buildings were also damaged by the fire.

52 How much does the newspaper cost?

53 How many times a week does the paper come out?

54 How old was Helen when she first became a firefighter?

55 What is the house number of the building where the fire started?

Look at the newspaper report. All of the numbers have been written as words. Can you answer these questions, giving your answers in figures?

56 How many firefighters tackled the blaze?

57 How old is Helen?

58 How long did it take the firefighters to put the fire out?

59 How many fires has Helen put out?

Safety First

Firefighters know what to do if they see a fire. Do you? If you see a fire, you should not try to put it out. Instead you need to raise the alarm. Shout "Fire! Fire!" very loudly and get out of the building as fast as you can. Then tell an adult or dial 999.

HOW DID IT START?

This block graph shows how some fires started.

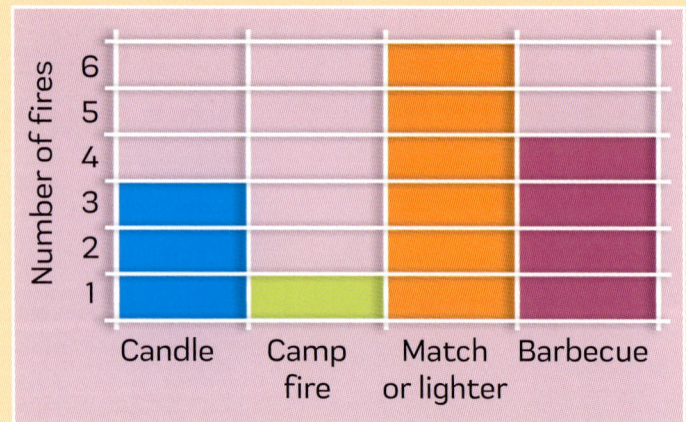

60 How many fires were caused by a match or lighter?

61 What is the total number of camp fire and barbecue fires?

62 What caused the fewest fires?

A   B   C   D

63 To stay safe we must read signs and understand what they mean. What shape are these signs?
A. danger!
B. read safety instructions below this sign
C. fire extinguisher
D. follow arrow to find fire exit

The gaps between the marks on the candle show one hour of burning time.

64 If you burned the candles in order, how long would it take to burn from the top to the bottom line?

65 If you lit both candles at the same time, how long would it then take to burn from the top to the bottom line?

Enjoy fires safely. Remember, firefighters are happiest when there are no fires for them to put out!

TIPS AND HELP

PAGES 6-7

Sharing and grouping: When we split a number into equal groups, each group is a fraction of the whole number. Here, each group is a team of firefighters.

Block graph: A block graph is a type of chart where we can compare two kinds of information. In this block graph, one block equals one fire, and the graph compares numbers of kinds of fire.

PAGES 8-9

Telling the time: When the shorter hand (or hour hand) is halfway between numbers on the clock and the longer hand (or minute hand) has gone halfway around the clock (when it is pointing to the six), we say the time is "half past."

Difference: Finding the difference is the same as subtracting. The difference between the numbers of fire hoses and the number of safety clothes can be written as 36−14. Remember, when you subtract, you put the larger number first.

PAGES 10-11

Groups of two: When working with groups of two, it helps to learn and memorise the pattern of counting in twos:
0 2 4 6 8 10 12 14 16 18 20 22 24

Following a map: It can help to follow a map if you turn the map to match the direction you are going. Turn the book around if you need to so that the road is facing the way you want to go.

PAGES 12-13

Half – The symbol for half is 1/2 which shows a '1', a line meaning 'shared by' and '2'. (One shared by two is a half).

PAGES 14-15

Compass points: N, S, E and W (North, South, East, and West) are the points of the compass. A compass shows which direction is north. It can help us find our way and talk about direction.

Pictogram: A chart where a picture is used to show one or more than one things. In this pictogram a flame picture means one fire.

PAGES 16-17

Number line: The ladder here is like a number line. It is as though there is a number on each rung. You can use the number line to count forward and back (or up and down the ladder).

PAGES 18-19

Naming shapes: To help name flat shapes, look at their sides and corners. Squares have four sides all the same length and four right angle corners. Rectangles have two pairs of sides the same length and four right angle corners. Triangles have three sides. Every point on a circle is the same distance from its center.

Scales: In maths, scales help read weighted measurements. We need to look very carefully to check that the measure is correct. For example, these scales show us kilograms (kg).

PAGES 20-21

Measuring with a ruler: Be careful to place the ruler so that the 0 (zero) is exactly on one end of the line to be measured. Then you can measure the width of the hose at the other end of the line.

PAGES 26-27

Words for numbers: Remember numbers can be written using words like "one, two, three" and using figures or symbols. We use just ten symbols to write all numbers. The symbols are 0 1 2 3 4 5 6 7 8 9. Where we put each symbol shows its value. So the one in the number 123 is one hundred, in 12 it is one ten and in 31 it is a single one.

PAGES 22-23

Clockwise: Clockwise is the direction the hands of a clock move around.
Anti-clockwise: anti-clockwise means the other way around, or opposite a clock.

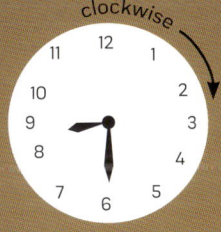

PAGES 28-29

Signs: It is important to be able to read signs. Spot them in buildings, in the street, and in your home. They are often warnings. Look also at their shape, as types of signs are often the same in shape.

PAGES 24-25

Reading a Table: When we collect information and write it in lists we call this a table. Here the lists are side by side, so we can compare them. In this table you can compare the four sets of hand weights.
Metres: There are 100 centimetres in a metre.

ANSWERS

PAGES 6-7
1. 8 people
2. 30 fires
3. 75 fires
4. 4 fires
5. 15 fires

PAGES 8-9
6. 3 days
7. 8:30 am
8. checking the engine
9. training
10. lunch
11. 22
12. 18

PAGES 10-11
13. A and E
14. 10
15. 6 minutes
16. C

PAGES 12-13
17. 6 vehicles
18. 6 miles
19. 90 times
20. fire engine
21. tree
22. 12
23. camp fire

PAGES 14-15
24. no
25. yes
26. camp fire
27. 9 fires
28. 11 trees

PAGES 16-17
29. 15 metres
30. Rung 2
31. Rung 8
32. 30 gallons
33. 9 hoses

PAGES 18-19
34. A triangle
    B rectangle
    C rectangles
    D square
    E circle
35. 8 minutes
36. 10 kg
37. 30 kg
38. right hand

PAGES 20-21
39. 1 yellow hose and 1 red hose, or 3 red hoses
40. 3 yellow hoses
41. 2 inches
42. C
43. 4.5 inches

PAGES 22-23
44. 6 rooms
45. anti-clockwise
46. 2
47. A = 13
    B = 4
    C = 20
    D = 2

PAGES 24-25
48. Set 3
49. 69 skips
55. 17 beats per minute
51. A true
    B false
    C false

PAGES 26-27
52. £1.50
53. twice a week
54. 23
55. 20
56. 9 firefighters
57. 26
58. 1 hour and 18 minutes
59. 48

PAGES 28-29
60. 6 fires
61. 5 fires
62. camp fire
63. A triangle
    B circle
    C square
    D rectangle
64. 9 hours
65. 5 hours

Printed in the China
A CIP catalog record for this book is available from the British Library.
All rights reserved. No part of this publication may be reproduced, copied, stored in a retrieval system, or transmitted in any form or by any means electronic, mechanical, photocopying, recording or otherwise without prior written permission of the copyright owner.

Picture credits
Shutterstock. 1: Anton Gvozdikov. 2-3: Gorodenkoff. 4-5: Eric Fahrner, Toa55, mon_ter, Simone Hoga, sandyman. 6-7: Tyler Olson. 8-9: Phichai, Flashon Studio, bogdan ionescu, mat27. 10-11: sripfoto, Monkey Business, Manuel Esteban, Rob Wilson. 12-13: AlexRoz, Rob Wilson. 14-15: macknima, KittyVector, tmicons.eps, Studio Barcelona, MMvector.eps. 16-17: NorSob.eps, StockPhotosLV, Toa55, John Kasawa. 18-19: Sean Thomforde, songpholt, Anatolir.eps. 20-201: TFoxFoto, Grigvovan, Arisha Ray Singh. 22-23: FXQuadro, JAANT, DedMit, Konstantin Faraktinov, Picsfive, Picsfive. 24-25: Monkey Business, SanchaiRat. 26-27: erikjohnphotography, Flipser.eps, MISHELLA. 28-29: My name is boy, lingdamphotothailand.eps, Arcady.eps, StockAppeal.eps, GulsevArtun.eps, GulsevArtun.eps, N-studio.

Every effort has been made to trace the copyright holders, and we apologize in advance for any unintentional omissions. We would be pleased to insert the appropriate acknowledgements in any subsequent edition of this publication.